Nathaniel,

Keep reaching

for the

stars!

from,

Ginger

Rudy

Rudy's New Human

For Daniel, Zelya, Jimmy, and Charlie

Rudy's New Human

Written by Roxanna Elden
Illustrated by Ginger Seehafer

Sky Pony Press
New York

Sky Pony Press books may be purchased in bulk at special discounts for sales promotion, corporate gifts, fund-raising, or educational purposes. Special editions can also be created to specifications. For details, contact the Special Sales Department, Sky Pony Press, 307 West 36th Street, 11th Floor, New York, NY 10018 or info@skyhorsepublishing.com.

Sky Pony® is a registered trademark of Skyhorse Publishing, Inc.®, a Delaware corporation.

Visit our website at www.skyponypress.com.

10 9 8 7 6 5 4 3 2 1

Manufactured in China, September 2015
This product conforms to CPSIA 2008

Library of Congress Cataloging-in-Publication Data

Elden, Roxanna.
  Rudy's new human / written by Roxanna Elden ; illustrated by Ginger Seehafer.
    pages cm
  Summary: Life was good for Rudy the dog—until the new baby arrived.
  ISBN 978-1-63450-189-7 (hardcover : alk. paper) [1. Dogs—Fiction. 2. Babies—Fiction.]
I. Seehafer, Ginger, illustrator. II. Title.
  PZ7.1.E4Ru 2016
  [E]—dc23
                          2014050074

Cover design by Sarah Brody
Cover illustration by Ginger Seehafer

Ebook ISBN: 978-1-63450-863-6

Hello, dog friends. My name is Rudy,
and I'm going to tell you a story, dog to dog.

If you are about to welcome a new human baby
into your family, you need to hear this.

Once, I was the smallest member of my family.

SQUEAK

SQUEAK

Life was good.

Then, one day, I heard some news. A new baby was on the way. (A baby is kind of like a puppy, but instead of a little dog, it's a little human.)

I was so excited to teach my new family member all of my favorite games.

But when the baby arrived, nothing was the way I had planned. The baby couldn't play the games I wanted to play.

And the games the baby did
want to play weren't much fun.

The baby definitely wasn't house trained.

And I like to get a lot of sleep,
but with the baby around? Forget it.

But the worst part of all was
that my family ignored me!

I didn't understand.
The baby didn't even know any tricks!

Be warned, friends: sometimes, having a new baby in the house can make you feel like you don't get any attention at all.

You have to learn to be patient.

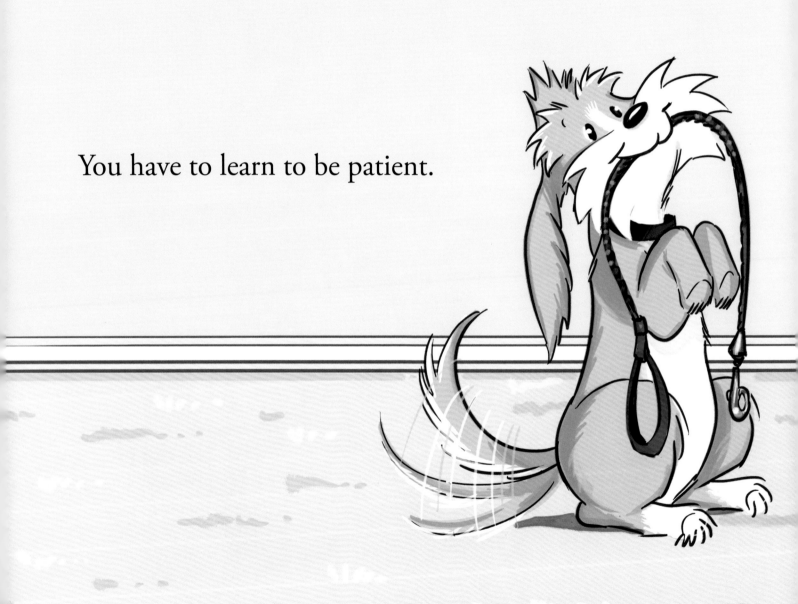

Walk!
Walk!
Walk!

Very patient.

And sometimes, you even
do things you're not proud of.

But there also are some fun things
about having a new baby in the family.

In fact, once you get used to it, having a baby in the house can be pretty nice.

I guess maybe there is enough attention for two of us.